Serving Love

BWWM Billionaire Romance

Norma Gibson

CONTENTS

Chapter 1

Tanya sighed, looking at her watch. Of course, it could be a ton of fun sometimes. Still though, today was one of those days where she would rather be at home, or at least doing something fun.

Her ebony skin tingled at the thought of getting out of here and curling up with her favorite romance book that she loved and adored. She knew that it would be nothing but a pipe dream, but hey, a girl could dream, right. She wondered if she would ever meet someone who could make her feel that way, or at least a prince that she knew and loved. She wanted that in her life, but it was hard for her.

For one, she wasn't into men of her race. She liked Caucasian men, and being an African American made the pool of potential suitors hard. Plus, she had a bit of a standard when it came to them, with the men being the type who would tickle her fancy, but also had a successful life going. She just wanted to have a relationship with a man, and ever since her ex, she hadn't met a man that really engaged her like he did. But of course, the two of them didn't really workout for one, mainly because he was so different. He was the type of guy who didn't want the romance, but rather just wanted to be in control. He was abusive and disgusting, not the type of man she wanted. But she didn't really have a choice until she got out of that relationship. That had been over a year ago, and now she wanted something new.

Tanya pushed her dark curls out of her face. That was all she wanted and needed, and she could tell she wasn't going to find that sort of thing in the library where she worked at. She might get lucky, but it was obvious that not many guys came into this type of place. This wasn't really the happing spot for romance, despite the fact that there was an entire section dedicated to it. Yeah, she knew she was shit out of luck, at least for now.

But she had to stay strong. She just had to. Her friend Mary came over, smiling at her.

"Don't look so down. It's going to be a great day," she said.

"You might say that, but I'm bored as piss right now," Tanya chirped.

"Well let's think of ways to make this place suck a little less. Maybe we can imagine the types of guys we want to come in. It would be fun," she replied.

Tanya rolled her eyes. She loved Mary, but that woman was such an idealist it wasn't even funny. Tanya wanted more than anything to tell her that it would be best if they just kept things to themselves.

But alas, Tanya knew that it was only going to get worse with wear. She hated working here, but she didn't really have any other choice. She did this for work-study, and she wanted to work as a history teacher, but this was the only thing that was open that was relevant to that. She wasn't going to forsake the job, but goddamn it was boring as shit. She would rather eat dirt than have to deal with half the shit that she dealt with on a daily basis.

Then it happened.

There was a presence in the library, a man who came inside. He was dressed in a neatly pressed suit, with brown hair that wisped over his eyes. He looked a bit older than Tanya, but with age came attraction, and she was attracted to that.

"Hello there," he said.

"Hello to you as well," she replied.

"Do you know where I can find the most recent texts on economics? I have a project that needs to be done, and I'm in dire need of trying to find some information on it," he said.

She blushed. This man was unlike anything she had ever met before. He was perfect, simply perfect, and she had to admit that it was probably the best thing ever.

"Oh yes. Come with me," Tanya replied.

She led him over to the area nearby, and soon they were alone. There was nobody around, and she could see that the man had a bit of a predatory look on his face. Did he really like her that much already? Maybe it was attraction at first sight.

"This is what we have," she said.

"Thank you. And might I say that you look delectable," he cooed.

She blushed, looking at him with a smile. "Thanks. So what's your name?" she asked.

"Franklin. And you?"

"Tanya. I work here as one of the librarians. I'm a student as well," she explained.

"Well that's cool. I hope you have fun with that. I have to say, I'm very interested in what you could teach me. Maybe you can give me a bit of a lesson," he said. The sultry nature of his voice made her feel like she was being sent into a tizzy. Tanya brace d herself, looking at him with a smile.

"Well maybe I can. But I have no idea when, because I would rather not do it in this public space," she said.

He moved closer, brushing up against her. His lips were right over hers, and she blushed.

"Well then come to my office tonight. I have a couple of personal things I would love to talk with you about," he said.

He gave her a card, and Tanya blushed. This man was so perfect, so sexy, and she felt like she was at a loss for words. He then pulled away, the space getting cold again but the desire in their bodies wanting more. She did want more from this man, and she could tell that it was only getting worse with time.

"Let's get out of here. I don't want you to get in trouble," he said.

"Fine Franklin," she said. She followed him out, and Mary was looking at them with a glance.

"All right, let me check you out," Tanya said.

"I know you've been doing that already," he breathed.

Tanya tried her best not to get flustered by the words this man uttered, but damn it was getting hard of hr. Of course, she wanted something else to get hard as well, but she was desperately trying to get her mind out of the gutter instead of keeping it there. She finished checking him out, and soon he was gone.

"Do you realize who that was?" Mary asked.

"Just a nice and extremely attractive guy named Franklin?" I asked.

"Wrong. He's only one of the biggest billionaires out there. His name is Franklin jones, and he totally has the hots for you," she said.

I blushed, realizing that name was a bit too familiar.

"Holy shit," I said.

"Yeah, and you should be careful. He does have a wife that would probably kill you if she found out about this," she said.

Tanya nodded, but her mind was more focused on the man at hand. Franklin was extremely attractive, and it sent her lions into a sopping mess. She would totally masturbate right now had it not been for the fact that she was at work. She would definitely have to go over there tonight, that's for sure. She could feel the anticipation in her body as she thought of the fact that she would get to be with him, and she wondered how intimate it would be. She kind of wanted it to be very intimate, but was a bit unsure. However, she would do whatever it took to be alone with him, that she was sure of.

A feeling of butterflies coursed over her for the rest of the day. She was going to see him. Plus, she had the address to his business, so she could go right in and they could continue where they left off.

A couple of hours had passed, and it was finally time to close. After Tanya made her rounds, Mary waited for her.

"Are you heading home?" she asked.

"No. I have business to attend to," Tanya replied.

Mary frowned, looking at her friend.

"I know you care a lot about this Tanya, but please don't do anything stupid. You might think that Franklin is a good man, but I just don't want you getting hurt," she explained.

I nodded, feeling a lump in my throat.

"Okay. But don't worry about me. I'll be fine," she said.

"Are you sure? Because you can't fool me," she said.

Tanya nodded. "Promise. Don't worry, I'll be careful when it comes to that man. I won't do anything stupid," she said.

"Fine. Have a good night," Mary simply replied.

She headed out, and Tanya headed to her car. She was going to see this man, and she would definitely have some fun tonight. It seemed like a good and liberating idea, and she didn't care what anyone else thought. She was happy with the circumstances, and she would definitely be happy with whatever would come next. Nothing would stop her, and she was definitely happy with the way things went.

Chapter 2

She got in her car and input the direction to the business. She was happy to have a GPS, because for a long time she didn't have one, and it made things awkward. She was happy to have it now, and once it was all programmed, she took off, the anticipation flooding through her. She was excited about this, and not just because it was a hot dude. She wanted this now more than ever because it would finally satisfy that craving she had for a man.

She knew that in a way it was wrong, but he seemed interested in her. She wondered what was going to happen, but she didn't know what to do. She decided to just wait for the situation to arise, and maybe she would be able to convince him to leave his wife. Judging from what Tanya read, he didn't seem all that interested in the bitch anyways, and maybe Tanya would be able to talk him out of being a scumbag towards women. She was just happy to actually have him around, so that's what made things okay with her.

She drove over to the building, which was an impressive structure that went all the way up. When she got inside, the receptionist looked at her with a wry glance.

"Hello there," she said.

"Hi. I'm here to see Franklin," Tanya said.

"Oh. Mr. Jones? He's up on the top floor. May I ask who you are?" she asked.

"Tanya. I'm here because I wanted to give him the information that he needed for the project he was working on. I working the library nearby," she replied.

The receptionist nodded, calling him and telling him what was going on. Tanya hoped more than anything the guy didn't forget about her. Maybe he just liked to play with women like that and she was going o get burned by him. But then the receptionist pulled away, looking at Tanya with a smile.

"He says you can go right up," she explained.

Tanya thanked her stars, heading towards the elevator and going to the top floor. She watched as the doors closed and she waited, the anticipation making her want even more. The elevator clicked all the way up, and she felt nervous as all hell. How was he going to react? What was going to happen to her? She was curious as well, so she waited until she was all the way to the top before stepping off.

The office was unlike anything she had seen before. Hell, the fact that he owned all of this sent a shiver down her spine. When she got to the stately door, she knocked, and suddenly, he appeared.

He had a relaxed face, and she smiled at him with a grin.

"Hello there," she said.

"Hey there. Glad you came. Come on in," he said.

She went inside, sitting down in the small meeting area that the place had. It was different, unlike anything she had ever experienced before. Most of the time, when she was in a place like this, most of the guys were just informal, but he was acting different. He seemed to want to act formal towards her, and she wondered what he was thinking about.

"So I take it you wanted to partake in the proposal that gave you?" he asked.

"Yes. I mean, you're really attractive and stuff and I wanted to get to know you better," she said.

"Very good. I'm Franklin. And as you know, this is my company," he said.

"I'm Tanya. I'm just a librarian," she replied.

"But you're a librarian with a nice booty. That's very important," he chirped.

She blushed, realizing what was going on. She wondered what he was going to think, and soon things changed.

"So you run this place?" she asked.

"That I do. And I'm happy to have finally found a hot piece of ass that's better than any I've seen in a while. See, I've been pretty…lonely so to speak, and I've been looking for the right woman. And I know that you're definitely one of the best I've seen," he said.

He slithered over to her, and she blushed in response. The way he talked was so docile, but it was full of passion that she honestly want' used to. She normally was the type to have a brief moment or two with a person, but then they would walk away. This man was dripping with lust and passion.

"So I guess you wanted men," she stated.

"Indeed. I want you very much my dear. Very very much," he replied.

She blushed at the way the words practically rolled off his tongue, and she wondered what else she could do in this situation. It was unlike anything she had ever felt before, and she could feel the anticipation in her bones. Before she knew it, his lips were right up against hers, and there was no way she would be able to resist.

A part of her mind told her that this was wrong, that she needed to stop, but this was different, very different, and she knew deep down that it was only getting better with time. She wondered what was going to happen next, but then, he did it.

He kissed her. He flat-out kissed her without any further goading. She was shocked, but he was a damn good kisser. She had some questions she wanted to ask him, especially about what this meant. He had a wife, and she wondered if his wife knew about them. But she wasn't going to bring that up right now, especially when it felt so good just to kiss this man. She wanted more, and so did he.

The two of them kissed for a long time, both of them refusing to move. She knew that he was delightful when it came to kissing; for the way he did so was almost like kissing something that you could be addicted to. Maybe she was addicted to his kisses already, she honestly didn't know. But the kisses were very nice, and it turned her on to no end. She started to let her lisp deepened it, and soon he was biting against her lip. She moaned a tiny bit, a small moan that was barely audible, but then he took that moment and used it to his advantage. He pushed his tongue into her mouth, kissing her and letting the wet muscle roam against her oral cavern.

It felt really good, that she had to admit. She let out a small sigh as he did this, realizing that he was pretty amazing at this. His tongue massaged all over her mouth, and soon it massaged against her lips. She let her tongue move against his, and she felt excited about things. It was definitely something she enjoyed, something that she wanted to continue to feel.

After a bit, he pushed her against the couch, climbing onto of her and overtaking her lips once again. His dominant nature made it practically impossible to do anything but follow his lead when it came to kisses, not that she minded of course.

She continued to kiss him senseless, knowing that she was completely under his spell.

He started to move his lisp downward, and she felt a small mewl escape her mouth. He then bit against her neck, and she felt a small yelp come out of her mouth once again. He pulled away, looking at her with a grin.

"You have to be quiet. We don't want anyone to hear us, right?" he said with a smile.

She nodded, feeling her body start to tense up with anticipation. What if someone did see them? The fact that it was possible did turn her on a little bit, but she kept those thoughts to herself. She didn't want to have that actually happen. But of course she was immediately pulled out of her thoughts by his lips as they started to lick and suck on the flesh of her neck. He did it gently, but the little touches with his lips were enough, and his breath warmed her up. She moaned, feeling her body crave more. He then made it all the way back down to where the edge of her collarbone was, trailing and tracing kisses against it. She could tell that he was debating between leaving a mark or not, but he chose not to. She smiled, feeling excited about the future.

He then pulled her up, and soon he practically tore off the vest and blouse that she was wearing. She was still in her work clothes, making her blush crimson as she thought about this, but he smiled.

"You looked damn hot in this when I first saw you. Now I get to see it off of you," he cooed.

The way he said those words got her panties completely wet. She never thought that he would be so damn excite about something like this. But then, he started to dart kisses all the way down her body, licking the orb of her breast and lightly teasing the area with his lips. She moaned, feeling her hips tighten and her pussy start to wetten. She knew for sure that he was enjoying this just as much as she was, and soon he got to the apex of her breasts, waiting a moment before he pulled away and undid the clasp on it.

She gasped as the garment started to slide off her body. He dominantly pulled off the shirt and bra, throwing it to the side. She was going to protest the rough nature of him handling her clothes, but then he started to dart kisses down her body once again, starting with the edge of her breast and going down to the tip of her nipple. He started to lick around the edge of the bud, making her moan and buck her hips in pleasure. He smiled letting his tongue curl over the area, teasing and tantalizing the puckered flesh, and soon she felt like her entire body was going crazy, begging for more than she has ever had before. She loved this, and she wanted it. He then started to let his tongue move up to the edge of her nipple, teasing and tormenting the area with his sultry lips for a bit before he started to suck on the little bud. She moaned, gasping out in desperation as she bucked her hips at the touch. It was so good, and son he was sucking on the flesh hard while his other hand made it was way over to the tip of her other nipple. He started to play and suck on them in earnest, and soon her body was craving more. The pleurae of the moment was practically too much for her, but she knew that her entire body was definitely getting what it wanted.

All of a sudden, he pulled away, lightly palming her nipples as a teasing measure. She whined, feeling a bit upset that he was done, but she knew what was coming next. He kissed down to her stomach, pulling her pants down as he did so, and she blushed at the way he was looking at her. She could see the lust and want in his eyes as he got to the edge of her pants, pulling them down along with her panties. Her glistening pussy was there for him, and soon he let his fingers tease and touch the edge of the area. She moaned, feeling her toes curl against the touches against her folds. He continued to probe, hitting the entrance of her pussy before starting to thrust his fingers in and out of her. She moaned, bucking her hips and letting her entire body start to shake with anticipation. He then started to push his fingers in and out of her faster and faster, digging deep and penetrating her hard. She was holding onto the couch for dear life, trying to bite her lip to keep from screaming out but utterly failing. By this point, she didn't care, and apparently Franklin didn't either.

He pulled away, grabbing Tanya and bringing her over to the desk. He pushed her against it, and she stood to it, spreading her legs and looking at him with a wanting glance.

"You like?" she asked.

"Very much so," he cooed.

He then started to undo his pants, pulling them down to reveal his aching cock. He was big, and soon he pushed himself deep into her. She gasped at the sudden feeling of his dick inside of her, but then she relaxed as she felt him start to completely fill her up. It was a bit shocking to her, but she liked it no less. He started to move in and out of her at a slow pace, and soon she was letting out small cries of pleasure as he did this. He loved the way that she sounded, and he praised her by slapping her on her ass while he continued to penetrate her hard. It was so good, and the raw desire that she had for the situation was starting to completely and utterly take over her. It was perfect, simply perfect, and she knew that he was getting into it just as she was.

She then felt him start to push his hips in and out of her faster and faster, and soon she felt her knees get weak with want. She wanted more, craved more, and after a moment or so, he penetrated her deep, hitting her sweet spot. She moaned, feeling her body tense up for a moment before she came hard, her pussy loving this. At that point, Franklin wasn't able to hold on to whatever he was trying to any longer, and soon he came as well, his seed spilling deep into her and filling her up. It was so good, and the pleasure was so raw. She felt her body start to tense up, feeling her hips shake and her pussy leak with anticipation as she came once again. Once that was finished, he pulled out of her, smiling.

"I take it that you liked that?" he asked.

"I did," she breathed.

"Good. I w thinking maybe you could come again tomorrow. I would love to get to know you better," he said with a smirk.

She blushed, realizing that he did like her a whole lot. She wondered what was going to happen next, but at the same time, she didn't really care. She got her clothes, heading out of there. But little did she know that the night of passion would turn into something that she didn't ever expect to happen, and something she wouldn't ever forget.

Chapter 3

For a while, things seemed kind of normal. She thought that maybe they would settle out with time, but apparently not. All of a sudden, thing started to change with her, and Tanya didn't know what was going on with her body.

For a bit, Franklin and her did start to hang out and have secret rendezvous. She wondered why he was able to stay so late without his wife knowing, but she didn't really know. He pretended like he didn't have a wife whenever they were together, which made it feel even stranger in a sense. She wanted to talk with him about that, to tell him that she was a tiny bit uncomfortable with the prospect of having to deal with a jealous wife because of their actions. Then, it happened. About three weeks after they started to have their secret affair, he started to feel strange. She brushed it off for a few more weeks, but by week six, the sickness got worse. Every single morning she would wake up, and Tanya felt like she was going to puke each and every time. She wondered what the hell it was, but she had no idea where it was coming from. Tanya looked around, trying to reason with the strange and new things that were happening, but she could only think of one reason for all of this shit.

Pregnancy.

There was no way she would be pregnant. She used protection with Franklin all the time. She was on birth control, and she made sure to take it. But then, the sickness got worse, and she was throwing up every single morning and felt tired nonstop. Then there were the cravings, which she had because she wasn't able to explain the feelings that she had. She wanted strange things, but nobody batted an eye. Even Mary didn't understand, but she knew and brushed it off as Tanya being weird again. Tanya was shocked at this, but she didn't know what else to do about it. Of course, she would wait a bit, but she didn't know what to really think.

Finally, she decided to bite the bullet and get a pregnancy test. If it was negative, then she wouldn't have to freak out anymore, right? It seemed like it was the logical thing to do, especially since she knew for sure that she definitely wasn't pregnant.

Or was she? She thought that she might be, but it might just be a stomach bug or something.

But sure enough, her worst nightmare had happened. She took the test, and it came up positive. She looked at the line that was on there, shaking with worry but also with a feeling of excitement.

She was going to be a mom.

She had no idea what the hell she was doing with that. There was something that she was worried about regarding this, and that was how he would react. She didn't know how he was going to approach this, or even if he would. A part of her wanted to talk to him about it, but another part made her feel sad. However, they had been talking of a while now.

She grabbed her phone, punching in the number of his business. She got the receptionist, who had a friendly tone of voice as per usual. She knew of Tanya, but rarely much about her. As the receptionist, it really wasn't her business as to what her boss did with other people, so she treated everyone the same way regardless.

"Hello?" she said. She could see the smile from here.

"Hi. Yes, I would like to speak with Franklin. This is Tanya. It's about a business proposal," she said. Tanya knew at this point that there was more going on than just a simple proposal, but what this chick didn't know wouldn't hurt her.

"Oh okay. Give it just a second," the receptionist replied.

She waited a bit, and finally, she heard Franklin on the other line.

"Hello there Tanya," he said with a sultry voice.

"Hey there. Listen, I have to talk to you about something. It's important. I mean, I don't think I can wait on this. Is there a chance that we can meet or something?" she asked.

"Yes we can. How about eight? I'm off then and we can meet up in the office," he said.

She knew that might be a bad thing, especially since she knew that many things have happened there. They've had sex there so many times; have had conversations that would only get passionate with time, and other such things. But she knew that this was a serious matter, and she knew that it had to be done.

"Okay," she said.

They hung up, and Tanya was shaking. She didn't want to tell him what had happened, but what other choice did she have? She was stuck in this rut, and it was only getting worse with wear. It's not like she could magically get an abortion or anything. Well she could, but she wanted to talk to him first.

She got ready to head on out, doing so and stepping into the building. It was quiet, so she made her way all the way up. When she got to the office, Franklin was there, smiling at her.

"Hello there buttercup," he said with a saccharine voice.

"Hey there. So we have a problem," Tanya started.

"What is it?" he ked.

She sat down across from him, grabbing the pregnancy test in a timid manner.

"I've been feeling strange over the last couple weeks, and I wanted to see why. I have no idea what was going on, I just thought I was sick. At least until I grabbed the test. I'm pregnant Franklin, and it's your child," she breathed.

Frank's disposition completely crumbled. He was in shock, looking at her with a glance.

"But I thought you were on the pill? You told me," he said.

"I am, but it failed," she replied.

"Shit," he said.

"Yeah, shit is right," she mused.

"Well there is more to this here than what meets the eye," he stated.

She looked at him, realizing what he meant. She knew that he did have a wife, but he never spoke of her. It was a sort of territory that neither of them trudged.

"What is it?" she asked.

"Well, that's something that I've failed to tell you. I'm sorry for doing so, but it's important to all of this," he stated.

She looked at him, gazing upon him.

"What is it?" she asked.

"I have a wife. Her name is Lauren. We're miserable together. I don't love her. I honestly haven't loved her for years. She's just with me because I didn't sign a pre-nup, and I know that she'll want half of it," he said.

"But what about us? I mean, I don't want to raise a child alone," she stated. She honestly was going to consider an abortion if she didn't get any help with it.

"That's the thing, I don't know what to do. I mean, I do like you a lot Tanya, and I want to raise this child with you, but there's her. There are her feelings I have to think about," he said.

"But you knew the risks when you had sex with me. Why are you backing out now?" she asked.

"Because I'm scared Tanya. I've built up this company from the ground up. I could lose it all and just get it all taken away in a moment. Hell, I don't know what to do about our situation. I've never impregnated someone before. I honestly thought I was sterile because Lauren could never get pregnant. But I'm scared to leave her," he said.

"So you would rather stay with a woman you don't even life over a woman you do like because of marriage? But you've already messed up the sanctity of it by being with me," she aid

"I know that," he said.

"So you're just throwing me to the side to save face. Wow," Tanya spat.

"I'm sorry, I don't know what to do," he replied.

Tanya was in shock. She couldn't believe this. She moved closer, looking at him in the eye.

"You know, I thought that I liked you because you were so strong and headfast. You acted like everything would be okay when we did this, and that you did it because you hate your wife. Well fuck you, because you're choosing to pussy out and ruin two people's lives, instead of saving one and being happy. Do you even like me?" she asked.

"Yes I do Tanya," he breathed.

She looked at him, a sickening feeling in her stomach. She can't raise a kid on her own. She knows that.

"Well I'm sorry, but I can't raise this child on my own," she said.

"I'm sorry. But I don't want to lose the child. It's ours," he replied.

"I know you think that, but you're just a sperm donor if you refuse to take responsibility for it. And honestly, I don't want to raise a child that was made with a man who is too much of a chicken to actually do something about this. You need to think about us, about the future, and if you're going to throw it all away, then I will a well. So what do you think?" she asked. Tanya wasn't going to have it.

He paused gulping at the feeling that was inside of him. He looked at her, his eyes heavy with tears.

"I'm sorry Tanya," he breathed. He was crying, but Tanya knew the answer. He can't give up the face saving that he is doing, but he is able to stay with a woman that he hates.

"You're pathetic," she spat.

Before he could say anything else to her, she got up, walking towards the door. Tanya felt bad, for she knew what she was going to have to do. She was going to have to abort it. She can't afford a billionaire's child, for she could barely take care of herself. She knew that it was for the greater good to get rid of the damn thing, but it still bothered her that it was even going this way. For now, she would just have to deal and figure out what to do in the meantime.

She didn't even look back as she left, for Tanya knew the answer. He was too worried about his own life to help take care of the life he created, so Tanya wasn't going to have to deal with that. She felt hurt, sad, and depressed, but Tanya knew deep down that it was for the best. She needed to do this, for she knew that it would save her life, and the lives around her later on.

Chapter 4

Tanya was crying when she went out to the car. He chose his wife that he hates over her, but he's completely okay with sticking his dick into her. God he was a pig, and Tanya realized that it wasn't worth it anymore. She knew that she wasn't going to be happy actually doing this, so she needed to make an appointment and get rid of it fat. It hurt her to think about it, but she would have to.

She called the local abortion clinic and asked for a consultation. It was for three days from now, so she took off work early to go to there. When she walked inside, she met with the doctors who were all friendly towards her.

"Hello there Tanya, have a seat," the head doctor said.

She sat down, looking at them with a glance.

"So tell me why you're here to get an abortion? Why don't you want your child?" she asked. She was a nice woman with strawberry blonde hair and blue eyes.

"Because I don't want to take care of the kid. I'm not financially and physically ready for it. Plus I got burned by the father. I don't even regard him as the father, but a sperm donor than anything," she admitted. Tanya felt sad about this, but she knew what was coming for her. She needed to get it out of her, for she knew that staying like this was only going to get worse.

"Okay, that makes sense. So have you had an abortion before?" she asked.

"No. I'm a bit scared honestly," Tanya replied.

"Don't worry. It's just a simple procedure. We take the cells out of your uterus. You will be knocked out, so you'll have one final say before we go through with it to opt out if you desire. But please, use protection for about a year afterwards. You're liable to get pregnant again," the doctor said.

She nodded, feeling nervous about all of this. She wondered if maybe there was some sort of way to opt out. Would she actually do that? Maybe, but she wasn't too sure.

She decided to make that appointment for a week from then. It gave Tanya enough time to actually think twice about this. She wondered if it was worth it to opt out, but at this point she didn't think so. The father refused to actually stay with her, but Tanya also felt like it wasn't fair to the child. Maybe the kid might grow up to actually be a decent person, unlike their father who gave up on her and instead would rather stay with a bitch they don't like. It bothered Tanya that he did that, but then again she kind of knew why. It was because she was black, and the baby was out of wedlock and considered cheating. Of course she didn't know for sure if that was the case, but it seemed like a dead ringer.

She hated to think about what she was doing, but she did frequently. Finally, when the day came, she felt sick to her stomach, but she got up and went over to the car, driving it to the clinic. When she got there, she changed into the gown, sitting there and waiting for them to wheel her in. She didn't feel confident about this anymore, but rather, she wondered if there was a reason for her to even go through with this. Maybe keeping the kid would be better for her, maybe not, but she was starting to feel uneasy.

One of the nurses came in, sitting across from her. Tanya called her in because she needed counsel, but she was starting to grow anxious.

"Are you okay?" the nurse asked.

"I guess. I'm scared honestly. I'm scared I'll make the wrong choice," she said.

"Well you did this because the guy was a scumbag and left you, right?" she asked.

"Yeah. We had a baby out of wedlock and he refuses to take responsibility," she said.

"Well has he tried to contact you since then?" the nurse asked.

She thought about it. He did once, but she ignored him. He did try texting her too.

"A few times but I never answered," she replied.

"Maybe he's changed. Honestly, this has happened before. The thing is, you got to think about yourself on this one. You're about to end the life of a child. I mean, I'm okay with doing it and being the one to help the doctors do so, but at the end of the day, you're the one who has to live with it. It's a loss, and it could be a big one. If you're not ready to go through with it, then don't do it. Otherwise, you'll be taken in about thirty minutes to the room where you will get to have all the fun of an abortion," she said.

Tanya thought about it. "True. But do you think he still cares?" she asked.

"He might. I mean, did he seem against you going through with this?" she asked.

"Yeah. He didn't want to leave the person he was with, but he cared about me. It was strange, but I've never seen a guy act like such a wuss before," she admitted.

"I have, and here's what I did. I would keep the baby, talk to him, and see if you can change things. If you can't, then come on back. But then again, I'm not the one who is in this position," the nurse explained.

Tanya agreed, but the woman did bring up a valid point. Maybe she was rushing into this too fast, and it was only getting worse with wear. She wondered what to do, but she could tell that it was getting harder with time.

"I think I might cancel," she said.

"Okay. I'll tell the doctors," the nurse said.

She placed her arm on Tanya's shoulder in a reassuring manner and left. Tanya got dressed, feeling a bit nervous about all of this. She needed to see him, to see the man that was important in her life. She knew that no matter what, Franklin would be the person she would need to talk to. Maybe he got his head out of his ass and she was able to finally talk to him about things. But then again, if he hadn't, then she would have to say goodbye to the baby. It hurt her to think about it, but she felt something inside of her practically beg for her to go see him. She didn't know what it was, but she definitely was ready to see where it would go. Maybe the truth was right out there in front of her face, and she just refused to look at it.

There was something telling her deep down to go back to his office and to see him. She felt a little weird about it, mainly after everything that had happened. When she got there everything was closed, but the door was open. When she got inside, she took the elevator in a gingerly manner all the way to the top floor, realizing what was going on. Things had changed, and it seemed like the place had almost an ominous atmosphere. She walked over to the door, knocking on it and waiting for the moment. She felt a struggling anticipation that started to erupt within her, and all of a sudden, he opened the door, looking at her with a smile.

"Hello there" he said.

"Hey there," she replied.

"Well I guess we should talk things out," he replied.

She walked in, watching him close the door. She could already feel a change in the atmosphere of this place, but she didn't know for sure what the hell it was. But there was something here, something that was different, and she knew that it would change the state of their relationship now, and forevermore.

Chapter 5

The two of them sat down on the couch, a bit awkward. Finally, Franklin spoke, looking at her directly in the eyes.

"So I wanted to talk to you. Did you get rid of the baby?" he asked.

She blushed, knowing that it was the first elephant in the room that they would talk about. She shook her head, gazing at him.

"I didn't," she replied.

"Why not?" he asked.

"Something was stopping me. It was almost like a force that was telling me not to do it for whatever reason that was. I had no idea what the force was that stopped me, but I did, and honestly I feel a bit relieved," she admitted.

"Good. I'm glad that you didn't," he said.

"Why are you glad? I get it it's your child, but you'll have to help me take care of it and pay for child support," she admitted.

"I know that you think it's going to be that way, but it's not," he replied.

She looked at him with a wondering glance. What the hell was he talking about? Why wasn't he able to actually see the changes here? Why couldn't he see that they weren't together, that he chose his wife over her, and they would be apart forever, not ever getting too close?

"What do you mean?" she asked. She knew that it was different, that's for sure.

"You think I'm still together with my wife, don't you?" he asked.

"Well yeah, I mean that's only the logical thing," she replied.

"I know you think that, but to be honest, you had quite the point when I talked to you that day. I stopped loving her a long time ago, and I don't want to stay with someone that I don't love. I've realized that the one I do love is you, and I don't need to stay in a bad relationship just to make myself feel better," he explained.

She nodded, feeling the desire start to course over her.

"Well I agree," she said.

"I agree too. And I love you Tanya. I realized that the love that I did have and the attachment was towards you. So I told Lauren that it was done right after we spoke. She hated me, threw me out, but my lawyer was able to only give her about ten percent, so the rest of the company and everything is mine. I let her keep the damn house because she wouldn't shut up about it, but I did buy another one. I actually wanted to see if you wanted to come live with me," he offered.

No way. This is practically too good to be true.

"That's amazing. I would love to," she admitted.

"Good. Because the thing is, I learned from you that it's okay to love others. I mean, I realized from all of this that the person I really loved is you. I want to take care of you, and our child. I don't want to get married of any of that crap yet, but I don't want to keep it just between you and the child either. I want you to have the child with me, and we can keep it a secret," he aid

"Wow, thank you," she said.

"No problem darling. And as for public face, I can say that you're a secretary and the kid is another's kid that you're taking care of. We can keep it on the down low until we're both ready to actually go into a new set of life," he said.

She agreed with that. She would still be in the limelight, but with him and she would get to keep the baby.

"I accept that," she said.

"Good. Because I want you to," he replied.

She blushed at those words, but before she could do anything, she felt her body gravitate towards him. The two of them looked at one another, their eyes feeling warm and bright against the other's face.

"You know, I've loved you for a while Tanya. You filled the void in my heart, and now that lure is gone, you're all mine," he said.

"Same here. I'm glad that you took a chance and stayed with me. It's by far the best feeling in the world. Thank you," she replied.

"You're very welcome. I love you Tanya," he said.

"I love you too Franklin," she spoke.

The two of them realized that love is what really mattered in the end. In a way, Tanya was happy she didn't throw out the baby and her life with him. Sure, it was going to be hard, but she knew that it was only getting better with time. She wondered as well what might happen to them next, but Tanya was sure that it would be nothing but good things.

"Thank you. For everything," Tanya said.

"You're very welcome," he replied.

The two of them let their lips move closer to each other's. She knew it probably want' the best thing in the world to do intimate things when pregnant, but she didn't care. They kissed, the taste of their lips flooding over them and making them both feel happy and excited for more. It was perfect to all of them, and she was happy about it as well. She continued to kiss him; feeling the lust and anticipation of the situation completely over take her. She felt her lips move and mingle against his own, her body relaxing against his. The two of them let their lips lightly bite and nip at one another, and soon they started to deepen the kiss. It got passionate fast, and the two of them were ready for more.

He started to snake his tongue towards the entrance of her mouth. She blushed, realizing what he was doing before letting him in. The two of them let their lips mingle with one another in a passionate dance that only they would know, and it was one that was better than anything they had ever experienced before. The way their lisp touched and their bodies mingled against one another was impressive, and it was better than anything they had ever felt before.

He pulled her up, bringing her to the edge of the cushion and onto his lap. He continued to kiss her, but he pulled off her clothing in a loving and passionate manner. It was different than before, which was a situation of him doing it simply because she was hot, or because of lust, but they had grown to love one another, care for one another, and the nights that they spent cuddling up next to one another were some of the best nights of her life. An s he kissed her, and soon after he pulled away and started to trail his lips downward, she realized that it was the perfect moment for her. She felt happy and satisfied that she had this man in her life, and it was only getting better from here.

She then started to feel him trail his lips down her neck, and she blushed as she felt the sanative tongue dart out and graze against her flesh. She moaned bucking her hips and loving the way that it felt. To her, it was heaven in a moment, and she wanted to make him happy as well.

She moved away, smiling at him as she started to do the same thing, taking off his jacket and shirt to reveal his chiseled chest. She played with his nipples, letting her hands dart all over them and causing him to let out a groan of pleasure. She palmed them, but then she got a great idea. Within moments, she moved her lips over one of the sensitive little buds, latching onto it before sucking on it hard.

She started off with some nice, even strokes, but then she started to move her lisp in a more fervent manner. It was one of his more sensitive spots, and she smiled in anticipation as she heard the man moan against her as she did this. It was nice, and kind of fun, so she continued it without any second thoughts. She loved how he was squirming under her, and she thought that it was kind of fun being the dominant one for once. She knew that it wasn't going to last forever, but she had one last thing that she wanted to do, and she was excited for it.

She moved her hands down, touching his taut muscles until she got to the edge of his pants. Without any second thoughts, she started to undo them, pulling them down to reveal his hardened member in his pants. She lightly grazed over it initially, causing him to moan in pleasure at the sensation. She continued to stroke it through the cloth of his boxers, smiling at him and his reactions. Seeing him acting lewd and turned on like this was the hottest thing ever, and she knew that he was excited. She continued his little actions for a bit, not caring about the tension that was present within.

She could see a small bead of precum exuding out of there, and soon she started to move her hands to the sides of his boxers, pulling them down in a slow and sensual way. He gasped, feeling his cock tighten at the feeling of her hands against the tip of it. She let her fingers dance over it, and he let out a groan. She smiled, starting to move her hands up and down against the head of his cock, smiling as he continued to groan in pleurae.

"Fuck," he breathed.

"You like?" she asked.

"Very much so. You're good," he stated.

She smirked, but then she picked up the pace. However, Tanya wanted to try something, to taste him to see what he was like.

She hadn't blown a guy in a very long time, but this was her chance. She got down, moving her face against the tip of his cock. She breathed out, and he groaned in desire. She started to take the tip of his cock in, touching and flicking over the head of his dick. She blushed as he started to groan and squirm, feeling his cock tense and throb within her mouth. She definitely loved that, and soon she started to suck on the head of his cock once again, teasing and touching the head and making him moan. She took him in deeper, feeling him start to moan against her once again as she took him even further into his mouth. She loved it, and he enjoyed it as well. She started to move her head up and down on it, starting from the tip and moving towards the center. It was nice, she had to admit, and seeing him groan and push his hips up was a sight to her. She continued to do this, moving until she got to the base of his cock and taking him all the way in. It was so good, and she enjoyed it. She then deep throated him for a little while, moving her head up and down for a bit until he moved her head away so as to prevent himself from coming.

"Fuck. That was good. Time to reward you now," he said with a smile.

He pushed her down, pulling her pants and shoes off. His hands gripped the sides of her panties, slipping them off to reveal her naked pussy. Her pussy was already sopping wet with want and desire and soon he was smiling, moving his lips over to the tip of her clit. He started to flick his lips over the tip of it, letting his tongue dart out to tease it as well. She let out a series of moans and mewls as he did this, bucking her hips and loving the way that it was going. He started to tease the rest of the area before moving downward and then touching the folds. They then continued to have fun with each other, for she started to let her hand move over to the edge of his cock while he continued to eat her out. The two of them were a complete tangle of limbs until he swatted her hand away. He wanted to give her some pleasure as well.

He started to tease the edge of her entrance, letting his tongue flick against her hole. She moaned, bucking her hips and loving the sensation that the man was giving her. He started to flick his tongue over the area faster and faster, loving the way that she was reacting to him. He then pushed it in deeper, hitting her sweet spot and loving how she was acting. It was perfect, and soon he pulled away, smiling at her before getting himself ready. He knew that they were ready for whatever action was about to come next, and Tanya definitely wanted this as well

He then started to move her legs apart, spreading them before he entered into her. He got in deep, and for a moment, the two of them stayed like that, joined as one and not doing anything else. He loved the way that it felt, and it was by far one of the most amazing feelings ever. He started to move in and out of her, and soon the two of them were moving as one. It was amazing, and she knew it. She knew that he was definitely having fun as well, and it was only getting better with time.

The two of them continued to let their bodies melt into one another, and they both knew how close the other was. It didn't take long at all, for they knew that neither of them was prone to lasting long after being worked up so much. After a couple more thrusts, she felt her body start to tense up, and Tanya's orgasm came over her. She screamed out, bucking her hips as her pussy tightened up, feeling her body start to shake with want and anticipation as she felt it completely and utterly overtake her and make her come hard.

At that point, Franklin was just about done as well. He let out a groan, pushing his cock deep within her, and soon he came inside of her once again, filling her up with his seed. The two of them waited a moment, locked in a passionate embrace that was unlike anything they had before. They realized they were in love, and nothing was going to stop them.

After he pulled out, he turned to her, smiling.

"That was good," he said.

"Sure was. I want to do that again with you. Now and forever," she replied.

"Well we will, because I divorced Lauren and I want to be with you. I know that it's going to be rough. Hell I don't even have a home right now. But I can assure you, I'll take care of you and the child, now and forever," he said.

"Same here. Thank you so much. I love you Franklin," she admitted.

"And I love you too Tanya. Always and forever," he said.

The two of them kissed once again, and she realized that it was only getting better and better. Her life did take a turn for the better, and she knew that they would be able to have the life that they've always wanted. He was happy, and she was happy as well, and she knew that no matter what came out of it, they would be able to live together forever, and nothing would stop them now.

The two of them knew that when they woke up they would need to figure out the future. It was obvious that they would probably have to spend some time determining what they were going to do with one another. It made them realize that it was going to be a hard road, but it was worth it. Tanya was probably going to have to quit her job, but they knew that it was okay. He decided to try to figure out how to get a new place soon enough.

After about a month or so, the two of them were settled into their new mansion. Tanya and him had a strong relationship with one another, and it was getting better with time. It was definitely something good, and the two of them knew that it was only a matter of time before they finally got their life together. But they both knew they had to do this, for themselves and for their child. It was going to be hard at first, but it was something that they would have to figure out now, and later on. They would do what they needed to do, and it was going to be okay. They had each other, and she knew that her man would be there for her no matter what.

--The END --

Here is a sample from <u>Loving The Tutor</u> story that you may enjoy:

… Belle couldn't breathe, but she didn't need to. All she needed was his lips on hers. All she wanted was to feel them press harder against her own. The world had melted away around them; there was only her and him. She stepped forward and closed the space between them, her chest rising and falling quickly against his. She could smell his aftershave; the scent filled her nose and intoxicated her brain with images of where the kiss might lead.

Sam felt Belle step forward, her chest was pressing against his, as his hands found their way to the small of her back. He let them rest there for a moment, putting just enough force in them to keep her close to him, but then he let them start to roam.

Belle could feel Sam's hands shifting from the small of her back. Every inch that they moved sent tingles up her spine and goose bumps to her skin. The kiss was still happening, expect it wasn't gentle anymore; both of them had a hunger behind it, both of them wanted more.

Sam pulled away gently after a second. The world came back into focus and Belle couldn't help but long for the kiss to be picked back up. She didn't say anything, she just waited for Sam to say something or do something…

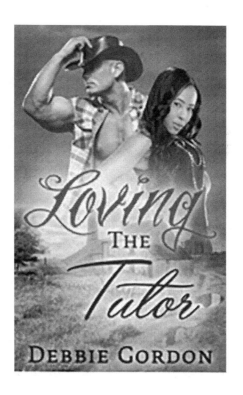

Loving The Tutor

Here is a sample from <u>The Cowboy's Stampede</u> story that you may enjoy:

"Excuse me? "I'm Anderson. Melissa Anderson. Are you from Brawler's Ranch?"

Ian turned towards the soft voice and felt his heart jump into his throat. In his front of him was the sexiest woman he'd ever seen. She had an 'I can handle my own' look about her, even though with heels on she only came up to his chest.

"Gotta go," he barked into the phone and clapped it shut. "I uh, I'm really sorry ma'am, I was expecting someone more-"

"More what?" She drew her eyebrows together, as if ready for the worse.

"Well, more manly. I mean man. I was expecting a man because the only name they gave me was Anderson." Ian's tan cheeks flushed a deep red before he remembered his manners and removed his hat.

"I'm Ian, Ian Brawler. Pleasure to meet you, Mrs. Anderson. "

Now it was Melissa's turn to blush. She wasn't expecting the billionaire himself to pick her up from the airport.

"Oh! It's Miss, actually, but you can call me Melissa. The pleasure is all mine!" She extended her hand to shake his. Ian juggled his sign and hat, only to have the cardboard clang to the floor. They both laughed at his fumble, and Ian brought his hand up to shake hers. As their fingers touched, a tingle ran through both them, starting from their palms and spreading all the way through their bodies. Ian and Melissa locked eyes, and couldn't help but smile at each other.

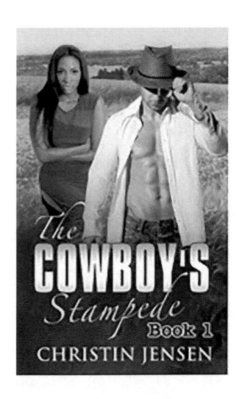

The Cowboy Stampede

Here is a sample from <u>The Cowboy's Redemption</u> story that you may enjoy:

...Well, at least he beeping made sense now. He couldn't see it—his neck wouldn't let him move his head that far—but he had no doubt now that it was a heart monitor, the constant announcement of his vitals remaining his only companion in this world of white and off-white. The pain in his chest became nearly biting after he let out a soft groan, making him grimace.

The sound of a door opening caught his attention, and the following footsteps made his attention pique. The curtain was pulled back, revealing a woman in a long white coat and green scrubs that was tell-tale of her position. Her skin was a dusty olive tone, which might have looked healthier in another scene and without such poor lighting. Her almond shaped eyes were dark and somewhat sunken, the effects of long nights and even longer days. She had a soft smile on her full lips and her hands were steady as she pulled a loose strand of thick black hair back over her ear where the rest of it gathered into a low ponytail behind her head.

"Glad to see you awake, mister Markus." …

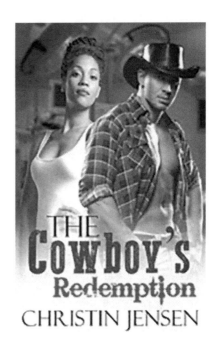

The Cowboy's Redemption